Miss Muglee Met Mr Get

Saker Mistri
Shaheen Mistri

illustrated by
Raju Devender
Sheetal Shah

assistant illustrators
Zamir Sayed
Rahul Patil

original character
illustration concept
June Watts Mistri

Supported by: JSW Foundation
          Wellwishers of the Akanksha Foundation

First Printing 2012

Price in India Rs. 250/-

Published by Arun K. Mehta for Vakils Feffer and Simons Pvt. Ltd.
Industry Manor, Appasaheb Marathe Marg,
Prabhadevi, Mumbai 400 025, India.

Printed by Bimal A. Mehta at Vakil & Sons Pvt. Ltd.
Industry Manor, Appasaheb Marathe Marg,
Prabhadevi, Mumbai 400 025, India.

ISBN No.: 978-81-8462-056-6

www.vakilspublications.com
info@vakilspublications.com
Phone: 91-22-2430 6780 / 2430 0609
Fax: 91-22-2422 5111

For
Mahir
Jihaan
Samara
Sana
and *all* the children.

In the state of Gujarat
Where the Gir forest grew,
Lived a peacock adorned
All in brilliant blue.

A hundred green circles
Glowed on his feathers,
Gleaming like emeralds
A-shine in wet weather.

A peacock so rich
You will not have met yet,
As this richest blue peacock
Who was named Mr Get.

Mr Get I regret
Was so proud and so greedy
He never, no *never*
Thought of the needy.

So Get was unhappy
He wore a deep frown.
In spite of his beauty,
He smiled upside down.

He was sad out of fear
Yes, *fear* (let's be clear)
He thought that his things
They would all disappear.

His glittering rings
And his fancy iPod,
His iPad and iPhone
So rad, and so mod!

Each time the fear came
Zing Zigity Zitch
His scaly, blue tail
It started to itch.
His neck and his shoulders
went twitchity-twitch.

His eyes started spacing
His mind started racing
His legs started pacing
Zing Zigity Zitch!

He'd think oh dear,
Oh dear, oh dear.

What if *all* this disappears?

From the city Mumbai
A fast train ride away,
Miss Muglee zipped in
For a quick three-day stay.

Muglee hugged her friend Get
Excited and pleased,
And together they went
To his House in the Trees.

The house it was fancy
The house it was grand,
With high tech new gadgets
And glorious fans.

So many new things
So easy to share,
"Get, *give* some away
A flamingo's out there."

And there quite scared
Poor Surkhi stood,
As bravely as
She thought she could.
She stumbled up
The narrow lane,
"Ouch!" she cried
With tummy pain.

"I'm so starved
I've tired feet,
Give me something
Small to eat."

"No" shrieked Get,
"No, no, no!"
"No" shrieked Get,
"Out you go!"

On hearing this
Miss Muglee jumped,
She picked up half a cake
"Come on, dear Get,"
She firmly said
"Give *this* for goodness sake!"

So with a frown
Lips going down,
Get took her advice
They gave Surkhi a piece of cake
And a bowl of curried rice.

"Oh *thank you*, Get," Miss Surkhi said,
"Tonight at home we'll all be fed."

That night Miss Muglee watched with glee
That Get's lips curled up sleepily,
And strange it was that Get's strong twitch
Stopped
And didn't itch itch itch.

The next day Get woke up to see
Someone fumbling with the key.
He stormed across the twig-made floor
Who dared to stand outside his door?

The door flung wide, and Surkhi stood
As bravely as she thought she could.
She asked for food, her head bent low
First Get thought, "No, no, no!"
But then he slyly said, "Helloooo!"

(I'll teach this bird a lesson yet.
She won't come back to me I bet.)
And with a sideways evil grin
He welcomed Surkhi Pinky in.

He'd make that Surkhi work today,
And take the heavy twigs away.
"Dear Bird, you look so very strong
Now take these sticks and run along!"

Miss Surkhi traveled to and fro
From where to where Get did not know.
She carried twigs in tidy piles
She must have walked for many miles.

And by the time the night was near
Zing Zigiti Zitch
Zing Zigiti Zitch
The room was bare, the twigs were clear
But Get still itched
In *itchy-fits*.

He itched all through the day and night,
An itch impossible to fight.
He itched all down his tail, you see
Scratchy-wat-chy itchy eeee
Ouch, this itch is *soooo itchy*!

Zing Zigiti Zitchi Zitchi Zitch
Oh, what an itch!
Oh, what an ITCH!

Finally a new day dawned
Muglee stretched and Muglee yawned.
"Come now Get, let's take a walk
Let's stretch your feathers over talk."
Rightee leftee heel and toe,
Through Gir forest they did go!

Get, he chatted chitter-chat
About getting this and getting that
He warned, "Be careful how you live
Be sure to get and not to give."

Miss Muglee said, "Get stop! Please stop!
Don't claw your way up to the top
This makes me fizzy-dizzy sick
You're up to greedy kinds of tricks."

The chitter-chatter didn't end
They walked to where the path did bend,
And in between a neem tree dome
They saw Get's twigs were now a home.

Miss Muglee said, "Lets peek inside,"
And when they did, their eyes went wide,
For sleeping on the hard, mud floor
Was Surkhi and flamingos four!

No furniture was in the room
Except a hand-made wooden broom.
No mobile phone, no emerald rings
No fancy clothes, no rad iThings.

And yet upon each pink bird's face,
A smile so wide, so full of grace.
And Get he saw...
Zing Zigity Zitch
That *no* flamingo seemed to itch.

Miss Muglee wiped a teary eye
(For even crocodiles do cry)
She gently said, "See, Get it's true
They have a home, because of you."

"But," said Get," If you look in
Those birds don't have a single thing
No chair to sit, no bed to sleep
Why don't we *make* them everything?"

All that day
And through the night
They gathered twigs
And tied them tight
Made of them a bed and chair,
Closets full of things to wear.

And when the birds bathed in the pool
(As birds will do before their school)
Get snuck the bed and chair inside
Miss Muglee turned to him with pride.

Surkhi Pinky's mum and dad
Could not believe the luck they had!
A feather bed, so soft and light
A rug woven with colours bright,
A chair for you, a chair for me,
Now they could *sit* when they had tea.

Muglee's heart went jumpy jump
Thumpy bumpy thumpy thump!
She saw that Get had learned to give
He'd learned another way to live.

They watched a while, then turned to go
Rightee leftee heel and toe.
And before as they left, Get turned to say,
"My itch has gone, *gone* away."

That night the Pinkys sat to pray
To thank God for this precious day
And Surkhi said " I wish *we* could...
I wish *we* could do something good."

Something Good

It's soon time for the Garba ball,
The most exciting dance of all!
But two poor creatures can not go,
And they are called the Ugly Foe.

Foe number one is stinky Boar,
The children call him Stink-a-saur.
And Porcupine is number two,
They call her Hokey Pokey Poo.

And so the invites never go,
To those they call the Ugly Foe.

Surkhi now knew what to do
They'd go to the Garba too.

"Let's make them dresses fit for queens
Hide Porc's quills so they're not seen.
Let's make a perfume of fresh rose
And spray Boar with a healthy dose."

So little time, so much to do,
Stitching dresses pink and blue.
Find some petals, crush a few
Make them both look shiny-new!

With many, sparkly things in tow,
They went to find the Ugly Foe.
Surkhi clutched tightly tight,
An invite for the Garba night.

"Knock, knock wake up!" Surkhi said
"You're going to the Garba Ball!"

Porc and Boar just rolled their eyes,
Not believing her at all.

Surkhi opened case on case
Of silken clothes, and bands of lace
Rhinestone belts and perfume sweet,
(Boar was clapping from his seat!)

"It's all for you," Miss Pinky said,
And laid them on their leafy bed
Boar's eyes, they opened wider-wide
Porc, she jumped from side to side.

"We have so many brand new things!"
Things quite fit for forest-kings.
No one now can ever say

Stink-a-saur must go away!
Hokey Pokey cannot stay!

The Garba square was shining bright
It was a diya lit delight.

All were dressed up in their best
To celebrate the dancing fest.
Every creature, green or brown
Was there to win the Garba Crown.

Music blared beyond the trees,
Lions gathered entry fees.
Muglee stood in creature queue,
Get was dressed in red and blue.

Seeing Surkhi at the dance
The lions shot a *get-out* glance.
One bared a scary toothy grin
Till Muglee tapped him on his chin
And Get said, "Let the pink bird in."

Wooden sticks went clatter clatter
Animals turned to chatter chatter.
Deer and lions swirled around
Clatter chatter clatter sound.

Muglee taught Porc how to dance
To twirl, to turn, to sway, to prance.
Surkhi's eyes they shone so bright
On his phone Boar captured sights.

Clatter chatter clatter sound,

Twirly
Swirly
Dance around.

Suddenly
The music stopped
A lion roared
A glass was dropped.
Miss Muglee turned in time to see
Poor Porc being thrown out angrily.

"Get out of here, you ugly fellow,"
A lion at the gate did bellow.

"You hokey-pokey useless thing.
  No pokey-pokes in here you'll bring!"

Before Miss Muglee blinked an eye
Get flew to a branch up high.
In peacock pitch he shrieked aloud
To silence the unruly crowd.

"Listen now to what I say,
Then decide if Porc can stay."

"Once I used to have an itch,"
Zing Zigiti Zitch
Zing Zigiti Zitch
"All day long I'd twitch twitch twitch,
An awful, well-deserved old itch."

Until Miss Muglee told me "Get,
About your itch you needn't fret
There's another way to live
Instead of getting learn to give.
And if you try to live that way
Your awful itch will go away."

"Do you know that our Wild Boar
The one you call a Stink-a-saur?
From whom your children run away
Feels so hurt he cannot play.

One day the poachers with their guns
Chased your cubs and made them run,
Boar used the stink you cannot stand
To save the lions in Gir land.

Do you know that porcupine
The one you threw out of the line,
The one you called the hokey poke
The spokey spiky pokey joke?

Over years she's bravely killed
Each cobra with her pokey quill,
And kept each scaly snake away
So you could live and not fall prey."

The lion raced out of the gate
Wondering if it was too late,
He bowed before the porcupine
And brought her back in through the line.

Do these look like foes to you?
Porc and Boar are friends so true.

There were cheers for Porc and Boar
The lion king stood up and roared,
"It's time now for the Garba crown
Animals, please settle down.
Let us now do what is right,
And crown Get on this special night."

The animals began to cheer
Surkhi wiped away a tear.

But then the cheers turned into frowns
As Get took *off* his shiny crown.
Fluttered his feathers, jiggled his head.
And proudly crowned Muglee instead!

"My friend has taught me how to give,
To know another way to live.

And I have learned the best thing yet ...

To Get is to Give,
And to Give is to Get."

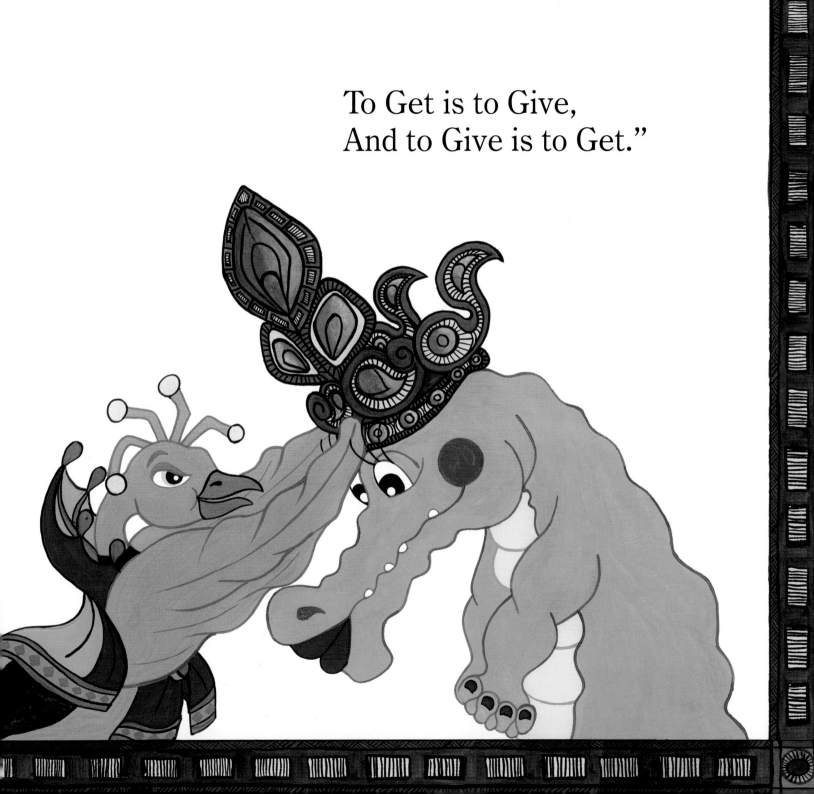

Boar and Porc were first to dance,
No longer stinky pokey prance.
Get and Surkhi sang out loud,
As they joined in with the crowd.

Muglee clapped her sticks with joy,
Dancing with each girl and boy.
The forest floor was now complete,
With every creature's happy feet.

The moon was bright, the night was long,
The stars twinkled with dance and song.
And all the lions stood in turn,
To offer thanks for what they'd learned.

Now in Gir where Get still lives,
They smile and say that *Get now Gives*.
His big wood door he opens wide,
And welcomes everyone inside.

And Get no longer has that itch,
Zing Zigiti Zitch
Zing Zigiti Zitch.

And Get no longer has that itch,
Zing Zigiti Zitch
Zing Zigiti Zitch.